For Richard McBrien

First American Edition, 1992

Library of Congress Cataloging-in-Publication Data
Allan, Nicholas.
Jesus' Christmas party / Nicholas Allan.
p.   cm.
Summary: Tells the story of the birth of Jesus
from the viewpoint of the innkeeper.
ISBN 0-679-82688-2 (trade)
1. Jesus Christ—Nativity—Juvenile literature.
[1. Jesus Christ—Nativity.]   I. Title.
BT315.2.A39 1991
232.92'1—dc20   91-17092

Printed in Hong Kong   10 9 8 7 6 5 4 3 2 1

There was nothing
the innkeeper liked
more than a good
night's sleep.

But that night there was
a knock at the door.

'No room,' said the innkeeper.
'But we're tired and have traveled
through night and day.'
'There's only the stable round the back.
Here's two blankets. Sign the register.'
So they signed it: 'Mary and Joseph.'

Then he shut the door,
climbed the stairs,
got into bed,
and went to sleep.

But then, later, there was
another knock at the door.

'Excuse me. I wonder if
you could lend us
another, smaller blanket?'

'There. One smaller blanket,'
said the innkeeper.

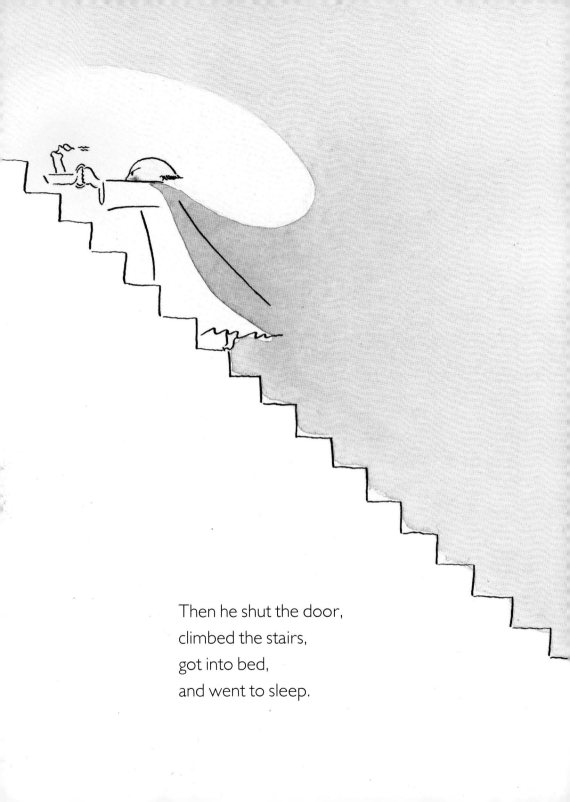

Then he shut the door,
climbed the stairs,
got into bed,
and went to sleep.

But then a bright light
woke him up.

'That's **all** I need,'
said the innkeeper.

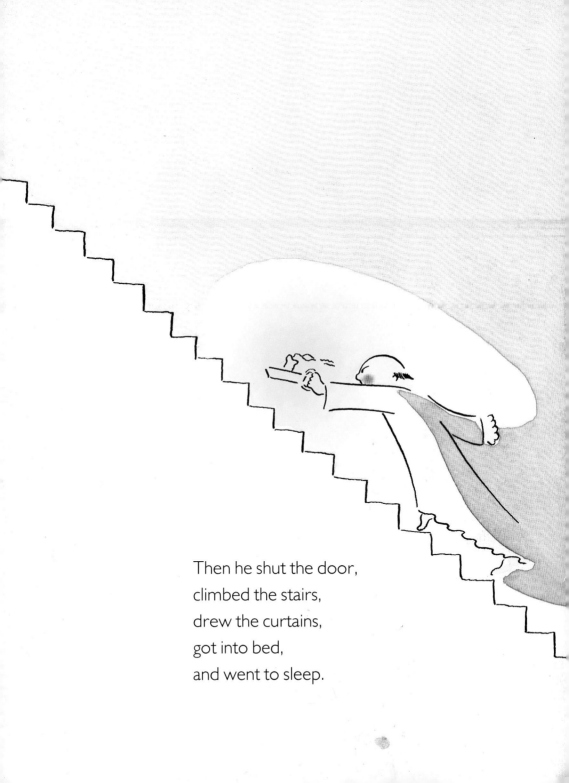

Then he shut the door,
climbed the stairs,
drew the curtains,
got into bed,
and went to sleep.

But then there was *another*
knock at the door.

'We are three shepherds.'

'Well, what's the matter? Lost your sheep?'

'We've come to see Mary and Joseph.'

'ROUND THE BACK,'

said the innkeeper.

Then he shut the door,
climbed the stairs,
got into bed,
and went to sleep.

But then there was yet
another knock at the door.

'We are three kings. We've come —'

'ROUND THE BACK!'

He slammed the door,
climbed the stairs,
got into bed,
and went to sleep.

But *then* a chorus of
singing woke him up.

'RIGHT – THAT DOES IT!'

So he got out of bed,

stomped down the stairs,

threw open the door,

went round the back,

stormed into the stable, and was just about to speak when —

'Ssshh!' whispered everybody,

'**Baby?**' said the innkeeper.

'Yes, a baby has this night been born.'

'Oh?' said the innkeeper, looking
crossly into the manger.

And just at that moment, suddenly,
amazingly, his anger seemed to fly away.
'Oh,' said the innkeeper, 'isn't he *lovely!*'

In fact, he thought he was so special . .

so that they could come and

. . he woke up **all** the guests at the inn,

have a look at the baby too.

So no one got much sleep that night!

THE END